E-I-E-I-O

How Old MacDonald Got His Farm

[with a Little Help from a Hen]

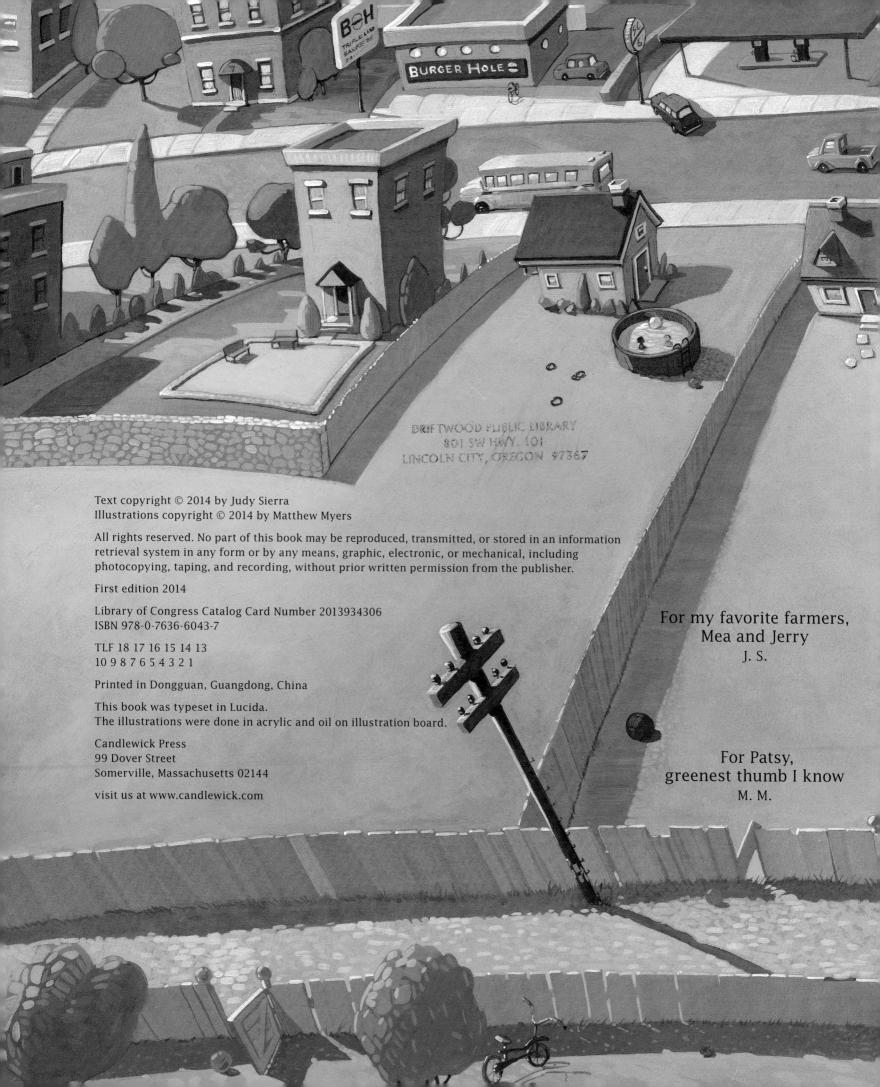

First edition 2014

Library of Congress Catalog Card Number 2013934306
ISBN 978-0-7636-6043-7

TLF 18 17 16 15 14 13
10 9 8 7 6 5 4 3 2 1

Printed in Dongguan, Guangdong, China

This book was typeset in Lucida.
The illustrations were done in acrylic and oil on illustration board.

Candlewick Press
99 Dover Street
Somerville, Massachusetts 02144

visit us at www.candlewick.com

For my favorite farmers,
Mea and Jerry
J. S.

For Patsy,
greenest thumb I know
M. M.

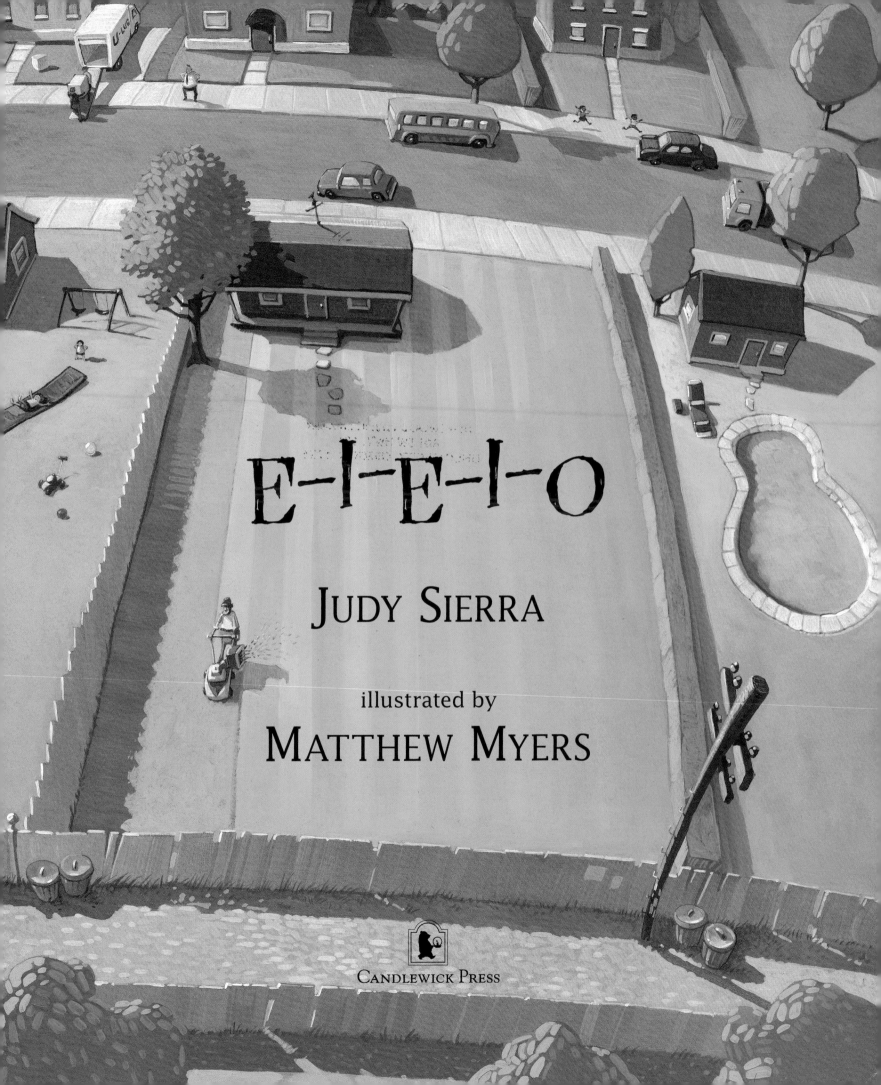

E-I-E-I-O

Judy Sierra

illustrated by

Matthew Myers

Candlewick Press

Old MacDonald had a house,

E-I-E-I-O!

Around that house there was a yard . . .

MOW

MOW

MOW

MOW

MO !

MacDonald said, "I love my yard,
but mowing grass is mighty hard."

So off he went to get a goat,

E-I-E-I-O!

The goat just nibbled at the edges.
Then she ate MacDonald's hedges!

Soon the plot began to thicken:
Old MacDonald got a chicken.
E-I-E-I-O!

Not your average bird was she,
but the smartest hen in history.

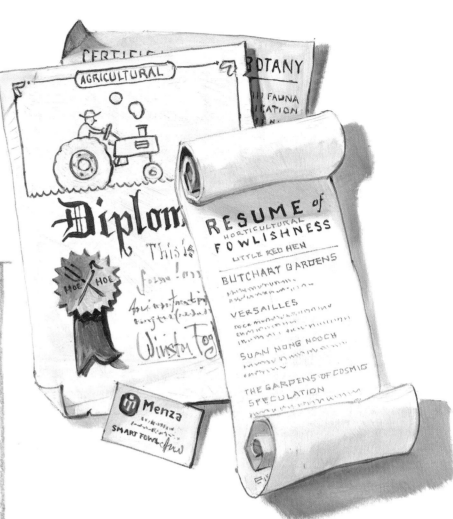

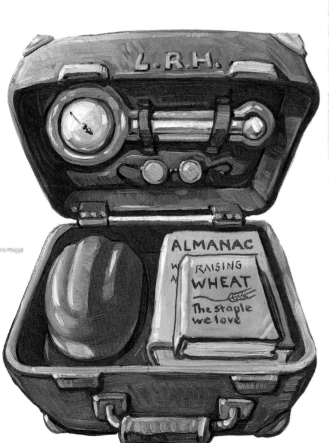

"Cheer up, Mac," said the Little Red Hen.
"You'll never mow the lawn again.

Join me in a garden caper—
cover up this grass with paper,
layer cardboard, then add dirt."

Mac tossed in his socks and shirt.

The rain poured down and made a flood.
MacDonald's yard was mired in mud.

The neighbors watched from up the alley,
then they held a protest rally.

The Little Red Hen got wet and wetter.
"Garbage," she cheeped, "will make things better!"

"Things could not get worse," groaned Mac.
He flung his food scraps out in back.

And when the mud had turned to goop,
the Little Red Hen, atop her coop,
clucked, "Who will help me find some poop?"

So Old MacDonald got a horse,

E-I-I-
E-I-
E-I-O!

KEEP ON THE GRASS
AMERICA
TINK TANK TUNK
GRASS SMELL BETTE
GOTTA GO
Come here often?
I'm your other end, noodle brain!
LES SPÉCIALS
LE POU-POU
filet
flambé
glacé

When the neighbors yelled,
"We hate that smell!"
Mac and the hen built a worm hotel.
In no time flat, those squirmy eaters
turned out compost, sweet and sweeter.

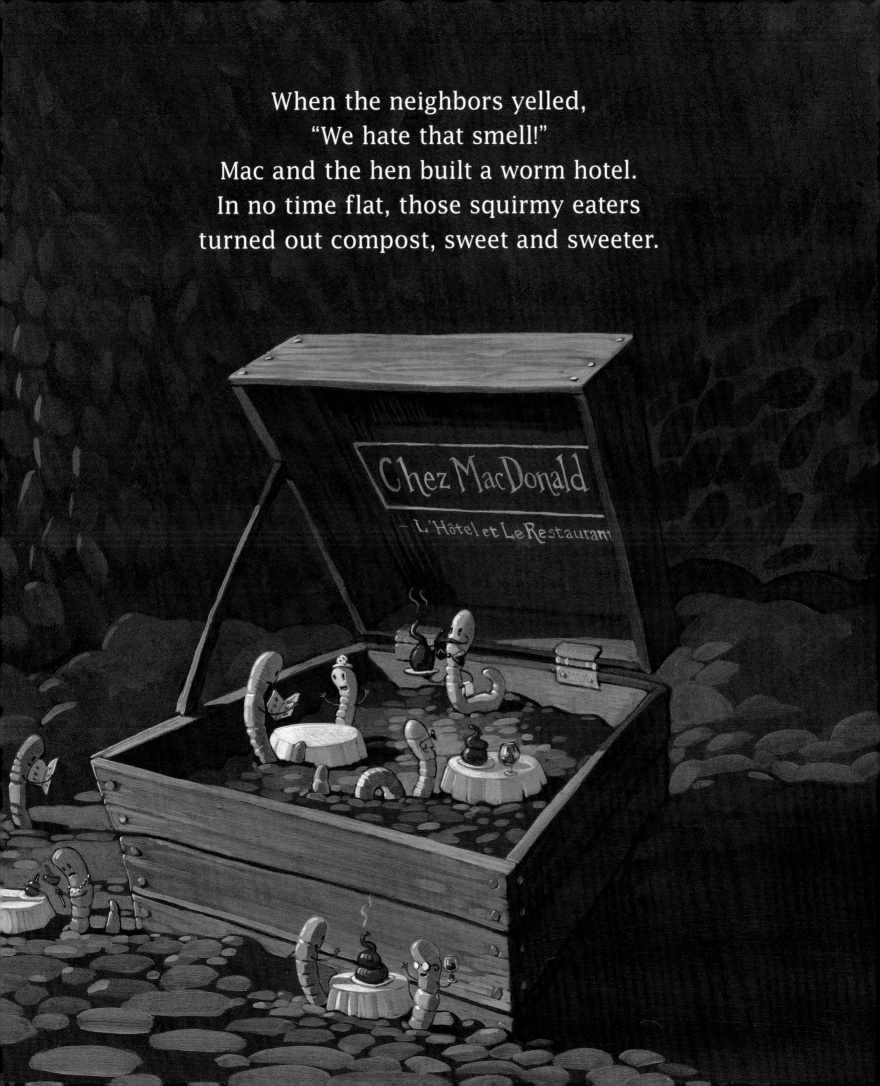

Gone was the grass;
gone were the weeds.

The worms churned, the sun beat down,
and magic happened underground.
Leaves burst out, and flowers too—
yellow, orange, purple, blue.
Then vegetables, so plump and sweet
that Mac had more than he could eat.

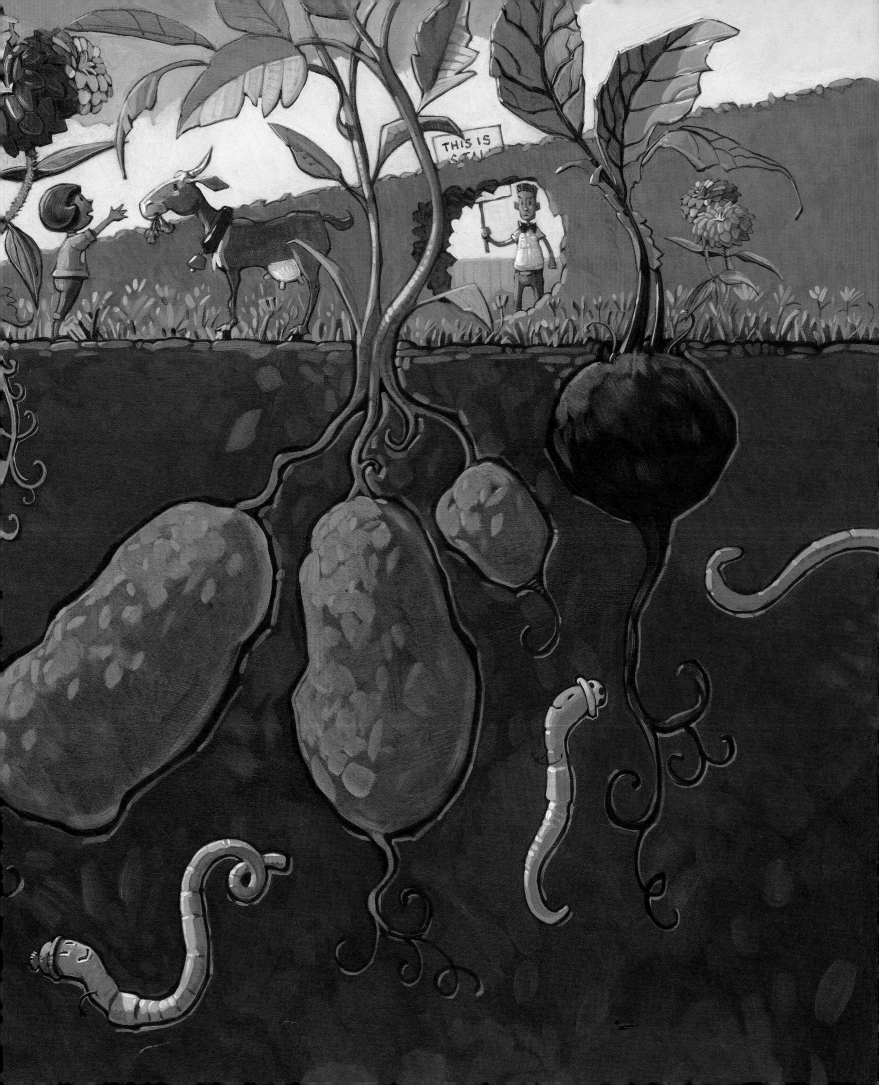

He milked the goat and made some cheese.
He traded eggs for a hive of bees.

The bees made honey,
and Mac made money.

And the neighbors said, "Mac sure is smart,"
as they bought fresh food from his garden cart.

Now Old MacDonald has a farm,
and he loves it so.
E-I-E-I-O!